Eulogy

More Than a Speech

Also by Stephen Outram

Books:
Public Speaking: Beyond Fear
Advanced Speaking Concepts
Wedding Speeches

Will Public Speaking Be The Death of You? (OOP)

Blog & Articles:
stephenoutram.com

Eulogy

More Than a Speech

By Stephen Outram

Author: Stephen Outram

Date Published: 1 February 2018

ISBN: 978-0-9943327-6-9

Publisher: Qest Press
PO Box 1770, Broadbeach, QLD. 4218. Australia

Cover Image
K|e|n|g. "Top View of a Dandelion.JPG." Wikimedia Commons, Angel Caboodle at English Wikipedia, May 2007, commons.wikimedia.org/wiki/File:Top_view_of_a_dandelion.JPG.

Contents

Preface

Eulogia, Ancient Wisdom

There have been a great many things said in my name over time, over centuries. Ever since there has been a need to acknowledge a life lived, I have been of service. You may know of me simply as a speech, but there is much you do not know. Thank you for coming to talk with me; very few do and I'm grateful.

I was officially recognised by the Greeks in the 15th Century as "eulogia" though the custom of praising people, living or dead, is old. From the earliest beginnings of humankind, when bodies have died, and entities embrace the great joy of death, I have been there, working with people like you, facilitating change and transformation from this reality to next. I know you all, I have touched you all in some way, I am old and yet never tire of my work. As long as humankind chooses to exist, there is no retirement for me.

My purpose and your purpose is to encourage the entity you have been tasked to speak of, to fully let go of this world and everything that they created within it. Acknowledging a life-lived, along with its creations and destructions, with care, gentle humour and no judgement, is a very fine gift. It is the judgement of a life-lived that can lock up an entity and cripple their choice to go. My job is, for just a moment or two, to create a space of no-judgement that includes everyone connected to the entity. And in that moment, invite them to another possibility, beyond this reality. Your job is to deliver the words, without judgement, and facilitate that. Without you I have no words, no delivery; without me, you have no capacity, but together and only together can our job be done.

You know of delivering a baby, a new body into the world, a new possibility for the entity with that body, well, Eulogy is very similar. We are delivering an entity who has been with a body, to being without one. The transition to and from bodies, can be difficult. Why do babies cry? Why do some entities remain, long after their bodies have died? While the funeral is for the living, it is Eulogy that facilitates the dead. Death's job comes first, then a funeral provides the gathering and Eulogy can be the entity's invitation to a new possibility. Eulogia, in praise, to laud, to flatter, to value and manipulate our entity over the line.

Yes! Manipulate! Using every trick in the book, every flattering phrase and word we know ... What? Do you think they want to go? Do you think they want to give up a lifetime's creation? Some will, but most will hang on for grim death! And so, our greatest caring and kindness is to trick them into choosing the great unknown, to leave the comfort of the familiar and to step off the cliff's edge, not knowing what will become of them. But we know; we know that they must step off to have what's next for them. The world they have left cannot embrace them without a body. It is similar to the zone that "customs" are, the border you must pass through to enter a country, you can't go back because

9

you have arrived, and you cannot enter until you present your passport. Except our entity does not have a passport, but they do have choice.

Have you heard that budgerigars who are born and raised in captivity know nothing but the cage, or fleas that are kept in a lidded jar will jump no higher when the lid is removed? The process of leaving their body, which they may have been living with, perhaps, for 80 or 90 years, is a similar experience for an entity. Given that that sensation and memory are experienced with the body, and you can see that an entity may be highly disorientated after death, that they may stay with the body they have left as it is familiar, that they will be there at the funeral with their body, and that they will be there for your address to them.

In times past, a body would lay in rest at the home of the entity for several days, where family and friends would come sit and talk with it, somehow knowing they were talking to the entity. This beautiful and caring process, often, would allow the entity to move on. It is sometimes called Sitting Up with the Dead or a Wake; for those of great fame or status it is called Lying in Repose or Lying in State. These traditions are less common these days and so, as Eulogy, you and I have more to do.

The first awareness you must have is that you are speaking to the entity. It will appear that you are addressing the gathering of living, but your words and our energy are for the entity. They are the one who are unsure of what is next, they are the one who do not get why they are outside their body, they are the one who cannot understand why no one can hear them, they are the one that we will guide to the cliff's edge and facilitate their first brave step, they are your unseen but not un-sensed audience of one.

Yours, in grateful contribution,
Eulogia

Introduction
Eulogy's Real Audience

There is a great deal written and said, viewpoints and opinions, about how you are supposed to do a Eulogy speech; fortunately, much of it is respectful albeit misguided. Eulogy has been adapted as a feature of funeral event-management, and funeral businesses now offer advice and tips on what to do so you can fit in to their plans. Their bias is towards providing the living with a great product experience and you can see this in the information, freely provided,

> "… of your memories, special moments together, your feelings for that person."

> "… it doesn't have to be their life story but more about what your loved one meant to you"

> "The most important thing is to write from your heart and express what means the most to you…"

You may notice that their advice is all about "you" and excludes the entity, who is your real audience. But a Eulogy speech is not a business product nor for the people attending, it is for the entity and this is the difference you can be, if you will choose it.

Do not make the mistake of taking the same tired and

worn, tricks and tips that are given to every customer; do not make the mistake of copying someone else's lines from a default template you find on the Internet, this is not for you or your entity. Your job with Eulogy is about you knowing what needs to be done, taking the lead; being a leader and facilitating the entity. If you will do this, the living audience will receive everything they require.

There are two key questions you can ask yourself:

1. Truth. What is really required of me with Eulogy?

2. What can I be and do to accomplish it?

What does the entity i.e. the person you've been asked to speak to, require so they will know their life is valued; that at least one person is acknowledging their creations and a life worth living. A father who brought his family to another country, an immigrant for example, may want to be acknowledged for his children now having a good education and jobs, and a new generation of grandchildren having greater possibilities. Perhaps the father's sole purpose in life was to relocate his family to a greater life in the new country. You will not find his story in someone else's story, my friend.

Or consider a young girl, whose religion discourages women accomplishing higher education, who overcomes all obstacles to become a PHD, and then dies. While the world will focus on the terrible tragedy of her young life cut-off short, she may have accomplished what she came here to do; to shine her spotlight on a different possibility for all women of her culture? She may be waiting, for someone like you, to simply acknowledge that, to value it. Will you look, beyond the drama of her death, and connect with the gift of her life?

So, it's not enough to copy and paste someone else's words, because those words were for another entity, to be delivered by another speaker; not you. You are being asked to contribute, you are being asked to speak and only you can speak as you.

And that is what is really being asked of you, that you speak as you … for there is no one else in the entire world who can do that. You have not been asked to speak because you are someone else, you were chosen because:

- you are You,

- you are trusted,

- you are valued,

- you have a unique contribution to make

- and you can do this.

In the following pages are guidance, ideas and suggestions; take what works for you and create your words, your speech, the one you will speak as only you can. Let's get to it.

The Eulogy Speech

A Gift Entrusted

The Eulogy speech is a very great gift that has been entrusted to you. In the main it serves to acknowledge the entity and facilitate them in moving on. In this regard you may never know if you succeed, and so you must gift it without expecting a result. This is one of the greatest gifts you can make, where you have no vestment in the outcome and you do not require anything in return.

In addition, Eulogy can allow the living audience to be grateful for this person they knew and what he or she created during life, which some of the audience may be a beneficiaries. It might remind them that they too are creating a life and have accomplishments, and they may become more grateful for themselves.

You many never know the full effect of your speech or what change it will create in the world, but know that if you will be its steward and allow it to be a true gift, it will create far beyond any purpose that you can imagine.

What to Include in Your Speech

If you follow through on the theme that Eulogy is for the entity, and it's possible that the entity is present, then you may consider asking questions. Put your attention on the energy of the entity and ask, for example:

- What do you require to hear?

- What can I speak of, for you?

And then ask of you, "What consciousness can I be to facilitate your choices?"

This technique is not designed to give you answers; it is more likely that you will experience greater ease in writing and delivering your speech. These questions can give you a different awareness beyond your own thoughts and points of view.

In addition to your own recollections and awareness, you can ask other people about the entity. Your questions will allow them to speak on aspects of the entity's life and inform your speech.

If you are privy to the entity's last will and testament, or a parting letter, there may be some items the entity has requested to be addressed that may inform your speech.

Another resource is the energy of the entity; the energetic imprint they made on the world will continue to exist for some time and you may be aware of it. This awareness is similar, for example, to when you buy a new car and suddenly, you begin seeing that same make and model on the road as your drive around; those cars were there before but you were not aware of them. When you choose to be the Eulogist, and connect with the entity's energy, you can have a different, expanded awareness and more can be available to you.

Here are some questions that may assist you in creating

Eulogy:

- What has [Name] accomplished with their life that they are proud of?

- What can I speak of to acknowledge [Name]'s creations?

- What does [Name] require that I can provide with my speech?

- Is there anything that [Name] has left unsaid that I can address on their behalf?

- What consciousness can I be to facilitate the greatest possible ease for [Name] and those gathered at the funeral?

- Who or what has information about [Name], and can I have that now please?

- What do I know about [Name], beyond what I think I know, that I haven't tapped into yet?

Writing a Speech
Pragmatic Tools That Work

Writing a speech is a way of getting all of your thoughts and ideas together in one place. Once refined, it provides you with an organized document that represents:

- what you would like to say

- what you must say

- and the order in which you will say it

From Non-Linear to Linear

One of the first things to do is to get all your ideas down on paper. The correctness of your grammar or spelling is not important here; just write. While you may be familiar with computers, there is something very useful about pen on paper, you can spread out many sheets of paper on your lounge floor and see everything at a glance; computer screens limit your view to one or two pages.

> "… for most of us we think in a non-linear way. The idea is to just get those ideas out of the head and into some sort of document, so that our ideas can be collected and organised. We have to be able to convert those nonlinear ideas into the

linear format that is a [speech]."—David Allen
Wizardgold, writer, artist

Review your ideas, move them around and then gather
them together in a draft order. You can use these pieces
of paper as a guide when creating your early typed
drafts, which will be further refined as you develop this
speech document.

Be aware that this valuable document is not your
speech; the speech is something that you will create
later, at the funeral with your audience.

A written speech can be made up of three top-level
categories and several subcategories. Identifying the
subcategories and the order they will appear, provides a
useful guide when creating the speech's content.

Connecting with Your Speech

Your speech is a creation, it's something you put energy
into; breathe life into and it comes alive in the world.
You give it a purpose, some words and then you share it
with others—it has a life force—and it may live on in
people's memories, on paper or perhaps a video. What
if, that life-force, can assist you?

Ask your speech what it would like to be; what opening
it would like to have. You may be surprised with what
your speech knows and is willing to contribute. Perhaps
you might say something like this:

"Hey, speech. So, here we are right at the beginning
and, you know, I have some ideas but I'm not that great
at speech writing. I haven't had a lot of experience at
speaking in public either. Will you assist me with all

19

this please? What do we start with? What can we write that will be the beginning of you and I connecting with the audience, with ease, and having an enjoyable time with it? What do you require of me and what do I require of you?"

With requests like this you are not seeking an answer to your questions; it is more that you allow an energy of contribution to flow into your world, and you begin receiving and being aware of more than you can by yourself. Your speech will contribute to you if you ask it. Will you?

It's Your Time

As a general guide, a Eulogy speech is around 3-5 minutes and a shorter duration of around 3 minutes may be appropriate. Check with the funeral organizer about your allocated timing. A lot can be said in 3 minutes and reviewing your speech against a time target will offer you the opportunity to refine it; particularly during rehearsal.

For a 5-minute speech, and in relationship to the next section, aim for:

- an opening of 1 minute

- a body of 3 minutes

- and a close of 1 minute

This is not a fixed proportion, so adjust it to suit your requirements; your speech.

Opening Up, Content & Close

1. The Opening

Just like an article headline or the cover of a book, your opening is an invitation that says, "Hey. Listen up friends. I have something important to talk about with you."

> "The headline is the most important copy on your page. It's the first message your visitor will see, and it has just one task: to stop visitors in their tracks."—Joanna Wiebe, Copy Hackers

The job of an opening is to get your audience's attention and keep it. It's likely that the funeral coordinator or priest will make space for you or call you up to talk; what you say and what you do in those first few moments sets the scene for what follows.

What invitation does your entity and audience require, that will allow them to be fully present with you and your speech?

Here are four ideas for opening:

1. Introduce the entity, for example,

"I'm here to reacquaint you with the life and times of John Jones and acknowledge a life well-lived. John was a husband, a father and above all, incredibly proud of his family and all that they have accomplished in the United States.

2. Ask the audience to participate, for example,

"Friends, will you join me in celebrating and applauding the extraordinary life of John Jones." then lead the applause, followed by your speech.

3. Ask a question, for example,

"How many of you knew John Jones well? Perhaps I can introduce you some areas of his life that are as great as he was humble, and as unknown as he was modest."

4. Share an interesting fact, for example,

"Did you know that out of the nearly 2 million people who emigrated from Italy in the 1950s, only a very few returned to their homeland. Such was the tenacity and determination of these people to create a new life in this country, and such a person was John Jones."

Dedicate a major portion of your speech-writing time to creating and crafting your opening; so that it can do its job and serve you well.

2. The Body

The body of your speech can be made up of several sections; subcategories that are chosen to assist you in outlining and then writing your speech. When you have a clear guide of what your speech will contain, it is much easier and quicker to produce the copy.

> "… that planning left me little to think about prior to writing. All I had to do each day was sit down and knock out that day's post, or part of the manuscript. I never had to sit and drum my fingers on the desk or scratch my head and wonder what I should write about."—Nina Amir, author

These subcategories are headings or the main points

you will be speaking about. The following chapter, The Eulogy Speech, contains information and suggestions that you can use as a guide, or allow them to contribute to your own ideas.

By working with several subcategories, the speech can be written in smaller, more easily handled pieces, rather than trying to write the whole speech from start to finish. The subcategories need to connect and flow from one to the other, so that the speech is smooth and your listeners don't need to make big mental jumps from one part to another (you'll notice this more acutely when you rehearse).

Use subcategories, as a flexible system of parts, to write up and organize the body of your speech. It is easy to insert new sections and shuffle the text so that the speech makes sense and flows, drawing your listeners on to the next piece of information, story or thank you.

3. The Closing

The closing is the last part of your speech and, in a sense, seeks to encapsulate what you have spoken about earlier; reminding listeners about what they have already heard. For example, if the body of your speech was a sequence of short stories about the entity; the last paragraph may be something like this:

"From the first brave step of immigrating to a different country, learning a new language, assimilating the culture, creating a business and supporting his family, John never lost sight of what his target was. He knew that if he could carve out a place for his children, then their children and their children's children would never again have to endure what he endured. And as

I look around this room, and see his legacy of happy, healthy grandchildren. John, if you're listening, I fully acknowledge your accomplishments and applaud your life's work. Well done, well done and well done."

In other situations, a close of this type leads to an important invitation; that of your audience responding and applauding, but Eulogy is different. Your close still invites their response, to reflect quietly, internally on what you have said. This is their contribution. So, make sure they know you're done and it's their turn. A simple "Thank you." may be all that is required.

The final part of the close is that it allows you to hand back the role of speaker to the next person, perhaps the priest or event organiser, and with that the focus comes of you and you can sit down.

Eulogy Speech Checklist

Be Sure

- My speech is written, with headings and notes

- My speech includes:

- An appropriate opening, suited to the event type, designed to get my audience's attention

- Special requests or mentions

- People I will be thanking

- …

- …

- I have rehearsed and I'm familiar with my speech

- I know the duration of my speech

- I have a printed paper copy of my speech

- My device is fully charged and loaded with my speech

- I know where the main parties are sitting

- I'm speaking from a: lectern, table, free-standing, stage, other …

- I've reviewed the venue and:

- checked on the venue lighting levels

- made myself familiar with the space

- done a sound check

- I know how to use the microphone

- I know when I'm speaking (order)

- I know who will call me, and whom I'll be handing over to, when I'm done

- Other ...

- ...

- ...

- ...

- ...

- ...

Speech Tools
Great Things to Know

The following pragmatic tools and techniques can be applied to the Eulogy speech and assist in its preparation, and in you having greater ease while you are speaking.

Your Cues Noted

At the venue the lighting may be low and there may be no lectern with a light. Your notes might be on a table well below your eyes with you trying to read them, glancing up to the audience and then back to your notes; make it easy to see and refer to your speech notes. If you know the lighting is going to be low, consider take a small battery-powered desk lamp with you.

Have your speech typed out in full and printed at a larger font size than you normally read at. Increase the size of each main section's headings to make them stand out; embolden the first word of each new paragraph. In addition, consider starting each new section on a new page or insert additional blank lines, so it is very clear where you are at in the speech.

Many people tend to rush through a speech; write in between the paragraphs, in big letters, the words, "Pause and Breathe" to remind you to take a deep breath and give the audience time to process your words, before you move on.

Include simple, words or phrases, highlighted, self-instructional notes that will assist you with your speech (format these to look different enough so that you don't read them out loud by mistake).

Power of Print

You may be familiar with laptops, iPads, cell phones, digital book readers and the like, but a printed paper speech will not fail you. It requires no batteries, is lightweight and easy to hold, the text will not freeze or disappear off-screen, the font will not suddenly become tiny as you swipe accidentally ... there are many good reason to have a good quality, printed paper speech to hand.

If you choose to go digital then have a printed paper copy of your speech with you, as backup, when you speak.

Dealing with Devices

If you prefer to speak from a device: smart phone, tablet, etc. make sure it is fully charged and you know how to use it.

Select a device appropriate for the job and for you, for example, if your eyesight in not strong then a tablet may serve you better than the small screen of a smart phone.

If you are using a phone, then turn off its speaker so that it's silent if someone rings you or you receive a message, mid-speech.

Humour

While it can be effective and entertaining, it's not a fixed rule to have humour in your speech. An interesting fact, inspirational poem or personal story, for example, will work well too. Given the nature of the event you are contributing to, it is not a requirement to be sombre either, lightness in your speech may be welcomed.

Be aware of what you create with your choice of humour when addressing a group of people. Many people do not do humour well; if you are one of them then consider not telling a joke or making light of someone.

If you do choose to include humorous sections in your speech, a self-deprecating (making fun of you) comment or story may work. Try it out in rehearsals; you will soon know.

What you think is amusing may not be reciprocated by your audience, and after delivering the punch line, you may get an uneasy silence. It is more likely that you will say something and unexpectedly sense a lightning in the room, without planning it. If this happens, then pause and allow your audience to experience their own sense of brevity.

Before you use humour, make sure it works. If do you tell a funny story, and it fails to raise a chuckle, then move on quickly. When you try to illicit or goad the response you want, following an attempt at humour, your audience may become confused or possibly resentful.

Even the Experienced Rehearse

Begin by reading your speech out loud to yourself. Check that it flows, is easy to read and change anywhere you stumble while reading it; simplify the languaging wherever possible.

When the speech works for you, get a yellow highlighter and mark the key sentences; the ones that clearly begin different parts of your speech. The section titles are obvious ones and look to mark those secondary starting points too, for example, where you describe an achievement or acknowledge a particular person.

Now, deliver your speech using only the highlighted lines as reference, looking up and speaking freely. If you get stuck, then refer to the body of the speech. You will quickly see where you are familiar with your speech and where you are not. Continue with this until you are familiar-with and have a connection-to everything you would like to say.

The idea is for you to speak from the headings, which will give you some space to speak directly with your audience; to look into their eyes and connect with the people you are speaking to. In this way you begin to include them in your speech rather than reading at them. When you include your audience, they will contribute in ways that you cannot imagine right now.

Get together with a friend or the other speakers and do speech rehearsals with them; get their feedback and adjust your presentation. If it's possible, go to the venue and run through your speech there.

Check the lighting levels and the layout of the room

you will be speaking in, whether you will be speaking from a lectern or free standing. Experiment the volume you will need to speak at to reach the far corners of the room, and then double it—when the room is full of bodies they will absorb some of your sound.

Mixing it with the Mic

If you will be using a microphone, then see if you can use it at the venue; listen to your voice through the speakers and get a sense of how you sound. Take the time to adjust the microphone's position to be close to your mouth and listen for the difference. A hand-held device often works well resting lightly on your chin.

Where are They?

Have a sketch plan of the venue ready and as guests enter the room, note where certain parties will be sitting, for example, the entities family, or someone you may be referring to in your speech. It can be helpful, if you will be mentioning someone in your speech and can look directly at them.

If you don't have a room map or cannot locate someone, then ask them to respond, for example, "Mary Black; where are you?"

Silent Applause

Eulogy, generally, is not applauded as per the normal hand clapping, but there will be applause for you. Your applause will more likely be the unspoken gratitude that the audience has for you, handling this task, and reacquainting them with the entity.

Those early moments, after you finish speaking, will

not be punctuated with a burst of sound, but the gentle, quiet energy of, "Thank you." Stay for a few moments and simply receive it.

Take One!

Many events are filmed and recorded. In fact, you may notice a plethora of smart phones, video cams, cameras and other devices, all pointing at you while you speak. You know that within minutes, some of these snaps or clips may be uploaded to social media websites. What do you do?

If you do not want to be recorded, then make it very clear at the beginning. Ask the event organiser to pass the word request that the guests honour your wishes.

If you are being filmed and photographed, then be you and be present with your live audience. Those filming are not really being present with you, so work with those people who are. Gift your speech to the people who are with you and allow the others their digital viewpoint.

Things You May Have to Handle
Being Aware of the Unexpected

A funeral or wake is a "live" event and some things are beyond the control of meticulous planning and organization. Here is a selection of some things that may come up for you before or during your speech. You may not have to handle any of them, but they are certainly good things to know about.

Expectation and Projection

Many, if not all members of your audience will have their points of view about what a Eulogy speech should be. They can project these upon you; they may judge you when you don't meet their expectations.

They may be projecting their grief, sadness, loss or tears, and expecting same in return. What if you are okay with the recent death and are simply grateful the entity was able to leave their body? What if you don't feel sad?

You must know that this speech has been entrusted to you, you are the one up there, you are the one in charge … Be You and do your job.

Emotion

During your speech you may experience intense emotion or the desire to cry; this can occur when you shift your attention off your audience and onto yourself. It is when you become involved in a story, event or memory rather than relating the story to others.

In addition, you are in a room full of people closely connected to you and your speech; is it possible that you are picking up on the emotion of others? Is it possible that your speech is working and actually creating an effect in the audience? Is that emotion really yours?

You can be aware of emotion and not buy into it as yours; just notice it. If it is very intense then take a moment, pause, drink some water, and then look up into the eyes of someone in the audience and put your attention on them; speak directly to them until you can speak easily and continue your speech.

> "Being vulnerable is having no barriers up. It is the barriers you put up, in defence, that prevent you connecting-with and receiving-from your audience. Vulnerability is one of the most inclusive and compelling experiences an audience can have, yet few speakers are willing to be the invitation that creates this being possible."—Stephen Outram, Advanced Speaking Concepts

Be willing to laugh at your tears, and acknowledge them. A speaker I know laughs through his tears and cries out, "I so hate it when I cry!" The audience laughs with him every time.

Laughter is similar to crying, and you may easily transition from one to the other and be able to continue.

Audiences will appreciate your honesty; your vulnerability when you take a moment to compose yourself. It gives them a moment too; perhaps you are all connected in the creation of this speech.

Lost for Words

It can be a very strange experience when you open your mouth to speak and you find your brain is blank and no words come out. Rather than panic, simply acknowledge it.

Look up and say something like, "On my, I've gone completely blank. Give me a second." And then refer to your speech notes and pick up on your speech again. It will be right there in your speech notes. You did print a paper copy out ... right?

Use Nerves to Advantage

Many people judge "nerves" as a bad thing and in so doing, use them against themselves but, are they really bad? Intense? Yes. But bad?

When you speak to one or two people it doesn't require much energy, but when you speak to 50 or 200 people then more energy is required. What you are calling nerves is the energy that you and your body have available, to be big enough to connect with all the people in your audience. Research has shown that when you embrace that energy, rather than trying to calm it down, you can speak better.

"I investigate an alternative strategy: reappraising anxiety as excitement. Compared with those who attempt to calm down, individuals who reappraise their anxious arousal as excitement feel more excited and perform better."—Alison Wood Brooks, excerpt from Advanced Speaking Concepts

It is your judgment of nerves that triggers your body's fight-flight-freeze system, which creates an unwanted reaction. By having a different viewpoint about nerves and acknowledging them as excitement, you invite different possibilities, give yourself other choices and can create a different result.

Forget a Name

Forgetting someone's name is not the worst thing you can do; not even close. You're in a room with many people, some you may have only met recently; no one is expecting you to remember all their names. Most people forget someone's name within seconds of being introduced! We all do it. When you are the speaker; the center of attention, everything seems magnified to you. You don't have to be perfect; just be you.

Just admit you can't remember, apologize. Ask them to tell you their name, for example, "I'm sorry. I've met so many people today and I've gone completely blank on your name ... will you remind me please?"

Feeling Sick

If you feel sick; nauseous, then do not ignore it until you are throwing up in public. If you are speaking and the sickness is intense, then hand back to the event organiser and attend to your body. Go and wash your face, drink some water and do what is necessary.

There may be another speaker who can step in, or you may be able to return later and do your speech.

Note: Your printed paper speech notes will assist the new speaker.

You, Drinking too Much

While, for some people, a drink may assist in calming nerves, be aware of what you create when you drink, and the effect alcohol has on you.

Handling Interruptions

Hopefully, at a funeral, you will not be interrupted, and the audience will be respectful. It is more likely that certain people may be overly noisy during the speech, whisper to each other, cry out in their grief, answer or interact with their smartphone, etc. The following may be useful in some situations:

Pause in your speech and invite the noisy, distracted ones to respect the occasion. Most will settle down after being singled out. Often, your audience will shush the noisy person long before you do.

If a telephone rings continue-on, or pause until they have taken their call outside. If they take the call, then ask them to move it outside.

If someone begins crying uncontrollably; loudly, then pause in your speech and allow it. If another member of your audience does not step-in to comfort the crier, or assist them outside, then ask, in a kindly way, "Can someone assist this person, please."

Someone Stands and Takes Over Your Speech

Given the nature of the event it is unlikely, but if it does occur then be in allowance of a member of your audience standing to speak. Your own words may trigger a memory, or inspire someone else to stand.

If they go on too long, then interrupt, thank them for their contribution and ask them to retake their seat. Most people will comply. While you are the speaker, know that you're in charge of your audience. It is totally appropriate for you to be in charge and invite their attention.

Order of Events
Who's on Next

Many events, including funerals, will have some semblance of tradition or organisation.

Here is a short list of possible speakers, with some notes:

- Family Member
  A member of the entity's family may speak to the gathering, perhaps to welcome them or thank them for attending.

- Eulogy
  The Eulogy speech is a recognized part of a funeral event and there will be a time set aside for it; there may be a program of events, which indicates when you will be required. Ask the event organizer or director.

- Friends or Colleagues
  People at the service may volunteer, impromptu, to speak. This may become drawn-out and emotional, and dominate the event. It may work better to invite them to share their thoughts and stories at an informal gathering, after the funeral service.

Resources

Beyond this Book

There are a great many resources that can assist you, beyond this book. Here's a short listing of some that will provide a broader view of the Eulogy.

How to Give a Eulogy by Tom Chairella

Chiarella, Tom. "How to Give a Eulogy." *Esquire*, Esquire, 8 Oct. 2017, www.esquire.com/lifestyle/how-to/a735/how-to-give-a-eulogy/.

The Science of Death: The Best Eulogy, According to a Physicist

Creighton, Jolene. "The Science of Death: The Best Eulogy, According to a Physicist." *Futurism*, 11 Dec. 2017, futurism.com/the-science-of-death-a-eulogy-from-a-physicist/.

Obama's Eulogy, Which Found Its Place in History

Kakutani, Michiko. "Obama's Eulogy, Which Found Its Place in History." *The New York Times*, The New York Times, 3 July 2015, www.nytimes.com/2015/07/04/arts/obamas-eulogy-which-found-its-place-in-history.htm

About The Author

Biography

Stephen Outram has a background of some 18 years in architecture, and since 1997 has worked as a graphic artist, website developer and Internet consultant. More recently he is a multi-book author, speaker and presenter.

Educated in Queensland, Australia, Stephen studied at Brisbane's University of Technology in the 1970s, then returned to study in 1995 at Dundee University, Scotland, achieving a Master of Science degree in Computing.

Stephen was an active member of Toastmasters International where he became President of Gold Coast Toastmasters Club, representing the club in speaking competitions and official events.

Stephen enjoys a diverse and wide range of projects including work, writing, music and song writing, boats and some sport. He is active with Surfrider Foundation Australia and is interested in sustainable and flourishing coastlines and waterways, free of plastics and pollution.

For more information, visit the website:

stephenoutram.com

Wedding Speeches

For many, being asked to give a Wedding Speech is the first time they will speak to a larger group, and these speeches may be done only once in a lifetime. Copying and pasting someone else's lines off the Internet is just not good enough. This book will assist you in creating your speech, with ease!

Professional speaker and coach Stephen Outram connects you with everything you need, to accomplish what may be one of the most important speeches of your life!

- Discover a simple idea with 3 parts and begin organizing and preparing your Wedding Speech.

- How to convert what's in your head, into a vital resource.

- Detail descriptions of the 5 key wedding speeches, including the Bride's Speech—a woman's role in transforming long-standing traditions

- The real job of a wedding speech and your role in accomplishing it

- 9 things that you may have to handle that no one tells you about!

Over 80 pages of information, ideas and techniques, designed to assist anyone who has been asked to give a Wedding Speech.

Public Speaking: Beyond Fear

Public Speaking: Beyond Fear is designed for people who experience difficulty with public speaking and performance. It will also benefit people who think they have it all handled.

The ideas, concepts and tools contained in this book may catapult you to levels of freedom and ease with public speaking that you've never had before.

- Begin functioning beyond normal

- Discover why anxiety is your best friend

- The weird, hidden issues that you can change

- The Art of Public Speaking explained

- Understanding Fight-Flight and working with your body

- Why amateur speakers never get paid

What if your journey with public speaking was really an adventure, unfolding before you with each new choice you make?

Advanced Speaking Concepts

Advanced Speaking Concepts is written for people who are seeking to create something greater and something different with public speaking. It will also benefit people who are beginning; the new generation of speakers.

This book contains ideas and concepts to assist you going beyond all of the old, worn public speaking techniques that everyone else uses to be competent, average and safe.

- Exposed! The myth that public speaking is the No.1 fear.

- The weird and hidden issues that are holding you back.

- Nerves! Why you need them to perform better.

- Applause. A beginning, not the end.

- Manipulation! Using it to advantage.

What if your journey with public speaking was really an adventure unfolding before you with each new choice you make?

More information at stephenoutram.com

Notes …

Notes …

Notes ...

Notes ...

Notes ...

Notes …

www.ingramcontent.com/pod-product-compliance
Lightning Source LLC
Chambersburg PA
CBHW050914120626
46552CB00004B/1567